D1256355

Topic: Environment and Life   **Subtopic:** Sound / Sound Pollution

Notes to Parents and Teachers:

As a child becomes more familiar reading books, it is important for him/her to rely on and use reading strategies more independently to help figure out words they do not know.

REMEMBER: PRAISE IS A GREAT MOTIVATOR!

Here are some praise points for beginning readers:

- I saw you get your mouth ready to say the first letter of that word.
- I like the way you used the picture to help you figure out that word.
- I noticed that you saw some sight words you knew how to read!

Book Ends for the Reader!

Here are some reminders before reading the text:

- Point to each word you read to make it match what you say.
- Use the picture for help.
- Look at and say the first letter sound of the word.
- Look for sight words that you know how to read in the story.
- Think about the story to see what word might make sense.

Words to Know Before You Read

desk

downstairs

drum

game

mower

sound

upstairs

wind

It's Too Noisy!

By Robert Rosen

Illustrated by Marcin Piwowarski

Rourke
Educational Media

rourkeeducationalmedia.com

Annie is downstairs. She wants to read.

What is that sound?
It's too noisy!

Put your drum away!

Annie goes upstairs. She sits at the desk.

What is that sound?
It's too noisy!

Stop playing that game.

Annie goes to the garden.
She opens her book.

What is that sound?
It's too noisy!

The mower is too loud.

Annie sits under a tree.

Oh, it is the leaves in the wind.

RUSTLE
RUSTLE
RUSTLE
RUSTLE
RUSTLE
RUSTLE
RUS

It is such a nice sound.

Now I can read.

Book Ends for the Reader

I know...

1. What did Annie hear when she was downstairs?

2. What did Annie hear when she was upstairs?

3. What did Annie hear when she went to the garden?

I think ...

1. Have you ever heard a noisy sound?

2. What was the noise you heard?

3. What is your favorite sound?

What happened in this book?

Look at each picture and talk about what happened in the story.

About the Author

Robert Rosen lives in South Korea with his wife, son and dog. He has taught kindergarten and elementary students since 2010. He likes to travel the world riding new roller coasters.

About the Illustrator

Marcin Piwowarski is self-taught in traditional as well as digital illustration. He managed to make over one thousand books during his twenty-year artistic journey. As a single father of three kids, he understands what to include in his art for it to be adored and eye-catching.

Library of Congress PCN Data

It's Too Noisy! / Robert Rosen

ISBN 978-1-68342-718-6 (hard cover)(alk.paper)
ISBN 978-1-68342-770-4 (soft cover)
ISBN 978-1-68342-822-0 (e-Book)
Library of Congress Control Number: 2017935434

Rourke Educational Media
Printed in the United States of America, North Mankato, Minnesota

www.rourkeeducationalmedia.com

Edited by: Debra Ankiel
Art direction and layout by: Rhea Magaro-Wallace
Cover and interior Illustrations by: Marcin Piwowarski